Flash Tickles the Keys

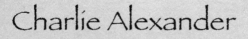

Charlie Alexander

Flash Tickles the Keys

By Charlie Alexander

Flash Tickles the Keys

Written by Charlie ALexander

Art Work by Charlie ALexander

Flash boarded the bus and
found many of his musician
friends.

He couldn't wait to see all the instruments
there would be at the concert hall.

"Here we are!" exclaimed Flash!

It was a beautiful building with lots of space and a big stage too.

The first performer was well known.

Everyone knew he would be an artist that would be hard to beat in a competition!

But the Giraffe was very accomplished too.

Flash thought they were both fantastic!

Even Santa came to audition!

He had practiced almost as much as Flash.

Practice! Practice! Practice!

Flash worked very hard to play well!

Flash loved to play the Piano.

The bench was very comfortable.

Flash had to practice his bow.

He wanted the audience to know that all the clapping made Flash very happy!

Flash dreamed about playing
in front of a big audience.

He hoped he played really good
even in his dream!

Flash thought he
might play the Violin.

Cello or Bass might be a nice
choice too.

"The Violin seemed to be the one I like" thought Flash.

But he wasn't sure.

The Bass Violin was a pleasure to play too.

It was hard to decide.

The Panda Bear had
already chosen the Cello.

Flash wanted to try other
instruments anyway.

It was so cool to see all of the musicians choose their instruments!

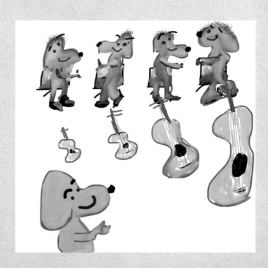

Flash decided to try other instruments too.

The Trumpet is a possibility.

But maybe a different choice.

Flash always liked sliding the arm of a Trombone.

But he still wasn't sure

It wasn't easy to choose! The Baritone Horn was nice too.

Maybe the answer was right around the corner!

The Elephant thought his trunk made a good Horn!

Flash wasn't so sure.

All the Brass instruments, including the French Horn were all taken.

Flash was in a hurry to try some Woodwind instruments.

The Oboe and the Bassoon and even the Flute were all gone too!

Flash was beginning to worry that all the instruments had a musician already.

Too bad the Flute
was already chosen.

He liked the Flute a lot!

Of course the Saxophone
was a temptation.

Flash thought he'd keep looking!

Wow! Bass Drum, cymbals, triangle and maybe Kettle Drums.

The Bells might be fun too.

Flash was right!

There were Kettle Drums.

Conducting the Orchestra needed a true leader!

Flash wasn't sure if that's what he wanted to do.

Then Flash saw a big black
Grand Piano!

I'm pretty sure that's the one for
Flash.

Flash had to choose which
Grand Piano he wanted to play.

There were three wonderful choices!

Flash had a good friend
to help him choose.

Flash found the Piano he wanted.

Playing the Piano was a dream come true.

Especially to play with the entire Orchestra!

Not even the Harp could change Flash's mind.

The Piano was the perfect instrument for Flash!

Flash loves to tickle the Keys best of all!

The End

To order additional copies of this book, contact:
Xlibris
844-714-8691
www.Xlibris.com
Orders@Xlibris.com

ISBN: Softcover   978-1-6698-6620-6
       Hardcover   978-1-6698-6621-3
       EBook   978-1-6698-6619-0

Library of Congress Control Number: 2023902239

Print information available on the last page

Rev. date: 04/13/2023

Printed in the United States
by Baker & Taylor Publisher Services